PIGS APLENTY, PIGS GALORE!

DAVID MCPHAIL

HARCOURT BRACE & COMPANY
Orlando   Atlanta   Austin   Boston   San Francisco   Chicago   Dallas   New York
Toronto   London

This edition is published by special arrangement

with Dutton Children's Books, a division of

Penguin Books USA Inc.

Grateful acknowledgment is made to

Dutton Children's Books, a division of Penguin Books USA Inc.

for permission to reprint *Pigs Aplenty, Pigs Galore!*

by David McPhail. Copyright © 1993 by David McPhail.

Printed in the United States of America

ISBN 0-15-307288-1

3 4 5 6 7 8 9 10   026   99 98 97

For Jack,
good friend, true poet

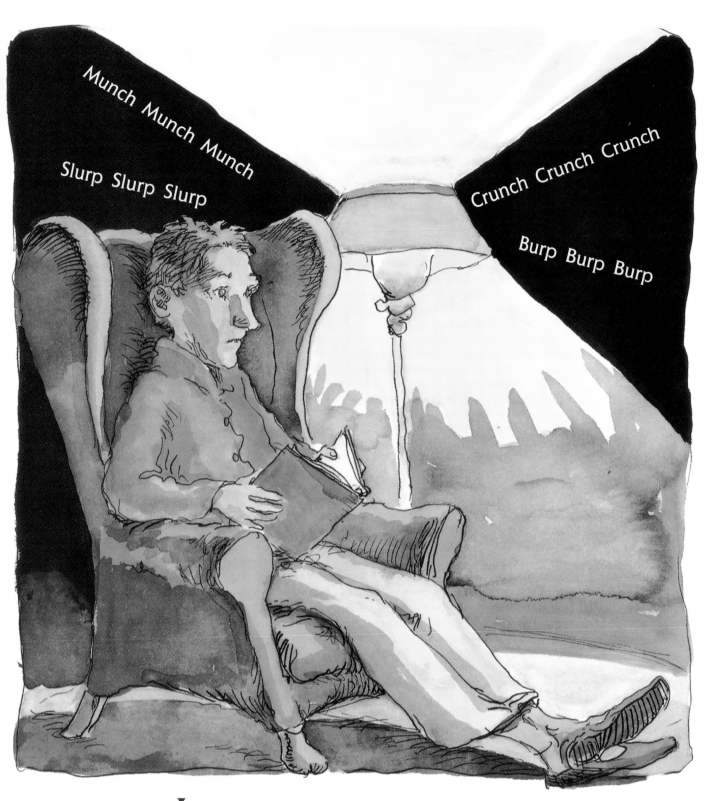

Late one night
As I sat reading,
I thought I heard
The sound of feeding.

Through the kitchen door
I crept,
Barely watching
Where I stepped.

A crash, a bang,
A shout, a yell—
I slipped on something,
Then I fell.

I landed on
A pile of pigs—
Some eating dates,
Some eating figs.

FIGS

Dates 43¢

In the cupboards,
On the floor—
Pigs aplenty,
Pigs galore!

Black pigs, white pigs,
Brown and pink pigs,
Making-oatmeal-
In-the-sink pigs.

Pigs in tutus,
Pigs in kilts,
Pigs on skateboards,
Pigs on stilts.

Pigs from England,
Pigs from France,
Pigs in just
Their underpants.

The King of Pigs,
The Piggy Queen—
The biggest pigs
I've ever seen.

Pigs arrive
By boat, by plane.
A bus pulls up
And then a train.

A band strikes up.
A piggy sings.
Then, at ten
The doorbell rings.

Someone yells:
"The pizza's here!"
And all the pigs
Begin to cheer.

Flying pizzas
Fill the air.
One goes SPLAT!
Against my chair.

The piggy piggies
Eat their fill.
I get nothing,
Just the bill.

BILL
50
PIZZA
£6857

"I've had enough!"
I scream and shout.
"Get out, you pigs!
You pigs, get out!"

"Please let us stay,"
The piggies cry.
"Don't make us go,
Don't say good-bye."

"You can stay,"
I tell them all.
"But sweep the floor
And scrub the wall."

I give them brooms,
A pail, a mop.
"Now sweep and scrub
Till I say stop."

The piggies work
And when they're done,
Upstairs they stagger
One by one.

They brush their teeth
And comb their tails,
Then wash their snouts
And clean their nails.

The pigs and I
Climb into bed.
I plump the pillows,
Plop my head.

I close my eyes
And try to sleep.
Before too long
I'm dreaming deep—

Of pigs and pigs
And pigs some more—
Of pigs aplenty,
Pigs galore!